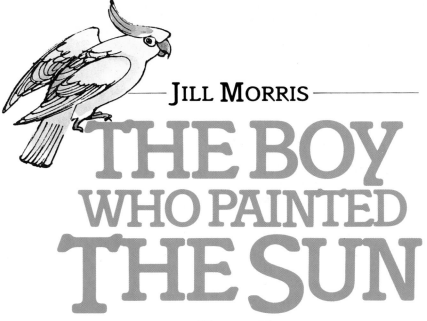

# JILL MORRIS

# THE BOY WHO PAINTED THE SUN

*Illustrated by*
## GEOFF HOCKING

From an original idea by Geoff Hocking

D1372485

To Nicolas and Alexandra
**G.H.**

To Henry Lawson, and to my mother, who first
introduced me to his works.
**J.M.**

Penguin Books Australia Ltd,
487 Maroondah Highway, P.O. Box 257
Ringwood, Victoria, 3134, Australia
Penguin Books Ltd,
Harmondsworth, Middlesex, England
Penguin Books,
40 West 23rd Street, New York, N.Y. 10010, U.S.A.
Penguin Books Canada Ltd,
2801 John Street, Markham, Ontario, Canada
Penguin Books (N.Z.) Ltd,
182-190 Wairau Road, Auckland 10, New Zealand

First published by Kestrel Books Australia, 1983
Published in Picture Puffins, 1985

Text copyright © Jill Morris, 1983
Illustrations copyright © Geoff Hocking, 1983

Made and printed in Singapore
by Tien Wah Press

All rights reserved. Except under the conditions described in the
Copyright Act 1968 and subsequent amendments, no part of this publication
may be reproduced, stored in a retrieval system, or transmitted in any
form or by any means, electronic, mechanical, photocopying, recording,
or otherwise, without the prior permission of the copyright owner.
Except in the United States of America, this book is sold subject to
the condition that it shall not, by way of trade or otherwise, be lent,
re-sold, hired out, or otherwise circulated without the publisher's
prior consent in any form of binding or cover other than that in which it
is published and without a similar condition including this condition
being imposed on the subsequent purchaser.

CIP

Morris, Jill, 1936–
The boy who painted the sun.

Previously published: Melbourne:
Kestrel Books, 1983.
ISBN 0 14 050544 X.

1. Children's stories, Australian. I. Hocking,
Geoff, 1947–   . II. Title.

A823'.3

**Published with the assistance of The Literature
Board of the Australia Council**

A boy lived on a farm

where there were some sheep,

and a brown dog who yapped at their heels and helped
to round them up,
and a tall grey horse which the boy hoped one day to ride.

There was a black and white cow,
and a tortoiseshell cat who kept her kittens hidden in the barn,

and some rusty-coloured bantam chickens who squawked and
fluttered in the golden hay.

In his room, through a crack in the wall, the boy could
see the sky.
Through a crack in the floor he could see the ground.
Flowers grew around his window and tried to come inside.

But times were hard. People were moving to the city.
The farm was sold.

The boy's family went to live in a cold, dark
building in a city street.

Next door there was a factory, then the gasworks fence.

The clangour of the city soon shut out the country
noises in his mind.

The boy sat on the doorstep and watched the sad faces as they shuffled past.

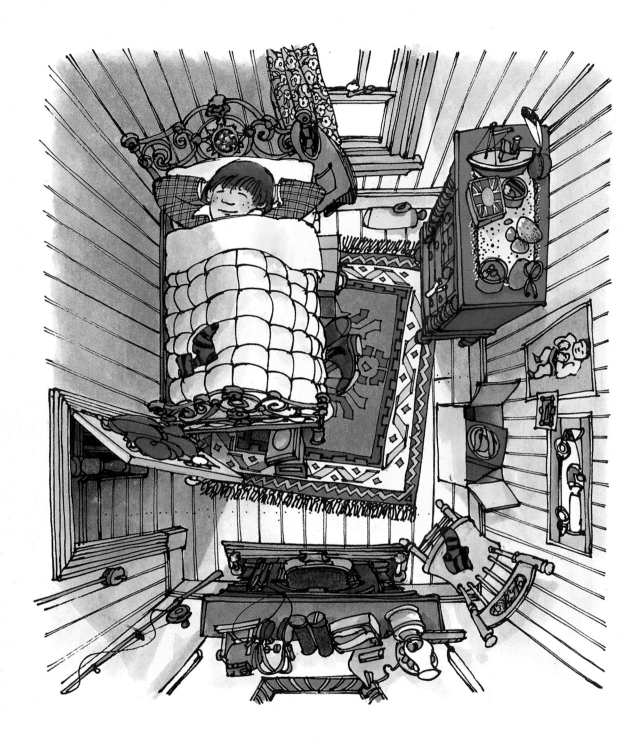

At last, he stayed in bed all day, with his eyes
tightly closed.

When he closed his eyes, he could see all the pictures
of the farm inside his head.

One day, a man came to the door.
He was selling matches and shoelaces and giant-sized
paintboxes nobody wanted to sell in the shops.

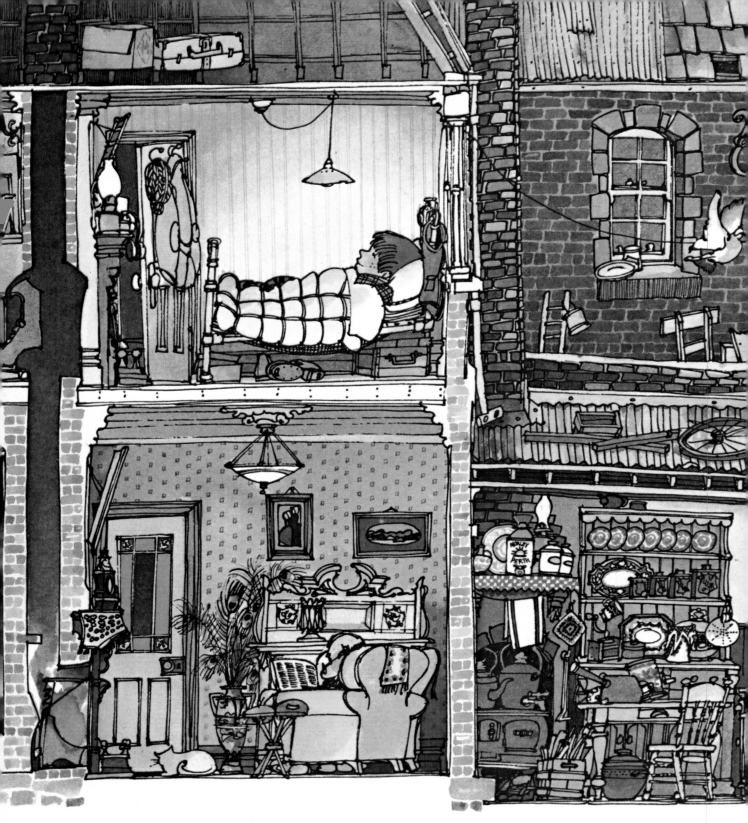

The boy's mother felt sorry for the man.
She bought a pair of shoelaces for her husband,
a box of matches to light the kitchen stove, and a
giant-sized paintbox to cheer up her son.

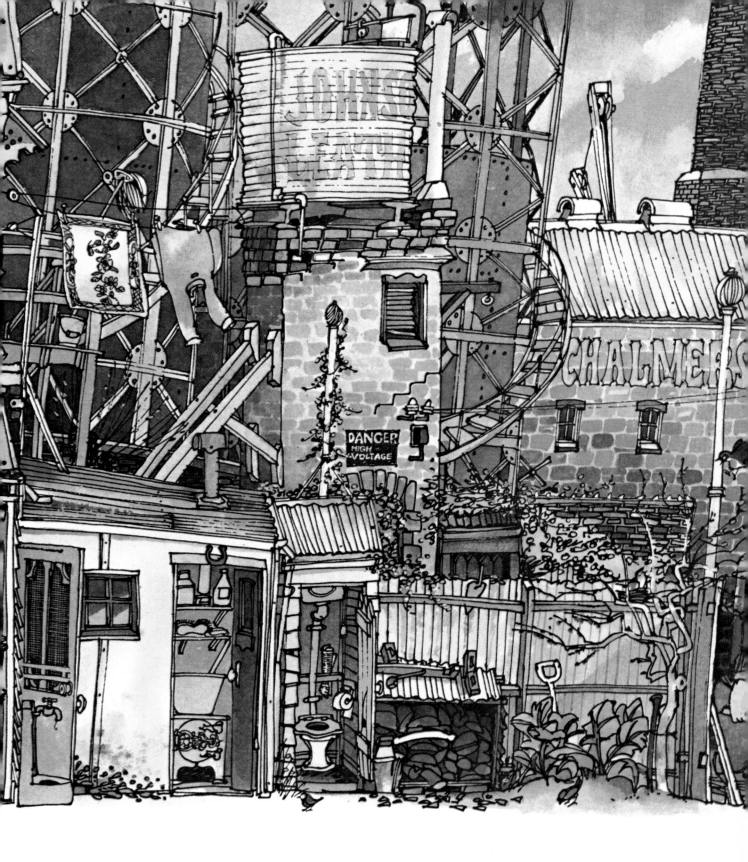

'Only tuppence-ha'penny, madam,' he said.

The boy opened his eyes to look at the colours inside.

His mother brought a pot of water and put it on the floor beside the bed. She spread out a piece of paper which had come wrapped around the meat.

'Paint me the moon,' she said.

The boy took the brush and dipped it into the water-pot. He chose a colour. And a flower grew on the paper, like the flowers which had grown around his window at the farm.

Alexander got out of bed.

He started painting flowers everywhere.

On the wall he painted a vine.

On the balcony outside, he painted trees.

On the factory wall, he painted some sheep,

and the brown dog who yapped at their heels
and helped to round them up,
and the tall grey horse he hoped one day to ride.

On the gasworks fence, he painted the black and white cow,
and the tortoiseshell cat who kept her kittens hidden in

the barn, and the rusty-coloured bantam chickens who squawked and fluttered in the golden hay.

Then he climbed up high
and painted the sun.

The boy's sun shone down on all the faces in the street
and turned their sad, grey looks to smiles.